Food +
Farming

FERGUS
TO THE
RESCUE

For Karin

Text and illustrations copyright © Tony Maddox, 2002

Designed by Louise Millar

Printed in Hong Kong
for the publishers Piccadilly Press Ltd,
5 Castle Road, London NW1 8PR

1 3 5 7 9 10 8 6 4 2

A catalogue record for this book is available from the British Library

ISBNs: 1 85340 771 2 paperback
1 85340 776 3 hardback

Tony Maddox lives in Worcestershire.
He has written ten books for Piccadilly Press including the seven FERGUS titles and SPIKE'S BEST NEST

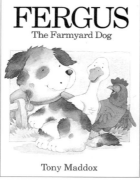
FERGUS THE FARMYARD DOG
ISBN: 1 85340 174 9 (p/b)

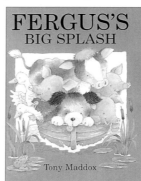
FERGUS'S BIG SPLASH
ISBN: 1 85340 388 1 (p/b)

FERGUS'S UPSIDE-DOWN DAY
ISBN: 1 85340 284 2 (p/b

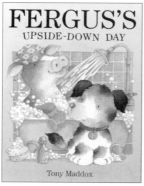
FERGUS AND MARIGOLD
ISBN: 1 85340 478 0 (p/b)

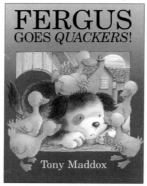
FERGUS GOES QUACKERS!
ISBN: 1 85340 566 3 (p/b)

FERGUS'S SCARY NIGHT
ISBN: 1 85340 631 7 (p/b)

FERGUS TO THE RESCUE

TONY MADDOX

Piccadilly Press • London

Summer was almost over.
Everyone had been helping load the hay.
Farmer Bob looked up at the dark clouds,
"Better hurry!" he said.
"Looks like we're in for a storm."

When the hay was safely stored,
Fergus found a comfortable spot in the barn
and settled down to sleep.
He was much too tired to go back to his kennel.

That night the storm came
and the rain poured down.
Fergus was glad he was
warm and safe in the barn.

Next morning Fergus woke to find the barn surrounded by water.
Farmer Bob drove up and shouted,
"Take care of the animals, Fergus!
I'll go and see what has happened!"

Fergus rounded up the animals and hurried them into the barn.

He counted everyone.
"One cow ... two ducks ... three pigs and four ...!"
WHERE WERE THE HENS?

Fergus ran outside and
called loudly . . .

WOOF WOOF WOOF!

In the distance he heard a faint

CLUCK CLUCK CLUCK!

He waded out towards the sound until he saw
the henhouse roof sticking up out of the water.
And there were the hens perched on top.
They were shivering with cold and looked
very scared.

"Cluck cluck cluck!" they called.

The water was now too deep for Fergus to reach them. He had to find something that would float. He rushed back to the barn. "Woof woof woof!"
Fergus told the animals of his plan to rescue the hens. They all agreed to help.

All they could find was a rusty bucket,

They carried them to the water's edge

some cooking pots and an old tin bath.

and tied them together with rope.

When the makeshift boat was ready, Fergus clambered aboard. With the ducks paddling, he set off to rescue the hens.

When the hens saw Fergus, they jumped up
and down and flapped their wings.
"We're here, Fergus! We're here!"
they clucked excitedly.

In no time at all, the hens were safely aboard Fergus's strange boat. On the way back, they also rescued a family of fieldmice, two very wet rabbits and a squirrel.

Farmer Bob was there to meet them.
"The river burst its bank," he explained.
"It's fixed now, so the farmyard will soon be back to normal."

They went back to the farmhouse to dry off and make buttered toast in front of the glowing fire. Farmer Bob's wife brought them hot chocolate.

"I think you've all earned it!" she said.